I0610140

M. A. B. (Mary Anna Buck) Evans

Nymphs, nixies and naiads

legends of the Rhine

M. A. B. (Mary Anna Buck) Evans

Nymphs, nixies and naiads
legends of the Rhine

ISBN/EAN: 9783337374679

Printed in Europe, USA, Canada, Australia, Japan

Cover: Foto ©Andreas Hilbeck / pixelio.de

More available books at **www.hansebooks.com**

NYMPHS, NIXIES
AND NAIADS

LEGENDS OF THE RHINE

BY

M. A. B. EVANS

AUTHOR OF "IN VARIOUS MOODS"

WITH ILLUSTRATIONS BY

WM. A. McCULLOUGH

G. P. PUTNAM'S SONS

NEW YORK   LONDON
27 West Twenty-third Street   24 Bedford Street, Strand

The Knickerbocker Press

1895

COPYRIGHT, 1895
BY
M. A. B. EVANS

The Knickerbocker Press, New Rochelle, N. Y.

TO
MY FATHER

CONTENTS.

ILLUSTRATIONS.

The following full-page illustrations, as well as the designs in the text, are from drawings by W. A. McCullough.

Nymphs, Nixies, and Naiads.

LEGENDS OF THE RHINE.

Nymphs, Nixies, and Naiads.

LEGENDS OF THE RHINE.

YE sprites and elves with which Germania's
    shore
Was thickly peopled in the days of yore,
Ye brownies, fairies, kobolds grim and gray,
And water-nymphs, disporting night and day,
Come in a host, and answer to my call.
Though unbelief has driven away you all
To hide in rocky caverns, sea, and cloud,
So that you dare not laugh or speak aloud
As in those merry days the world was young,
And people smiled and jested, laughed and
    sung,
Without these groanings of the inner sense,
These metaphysical discussions dense,
O'erawing, puzzling, darkening our life,
And making it with such vexed questions rife
As in these latter days attack our brains.
Ah ! then it was enough to live.   The rains
Of heaven were sweet, the sunshine passing
    fair,

13

While all about, in sea, and earth, and air,
Peeped forth th' ideal world, which we in vain
Strive after now, with heavy heart and brain.
    The world has grown too old, or else
        too wise.
    A veil has fallen over learned eyes,
    And lack of faith has chilled.   But
        just once more
        Come forth, O fays, and scatter
            blessings o'er
        A band of earnest seekers after all
        The higher joys, as well as those
            which fall
            More easily within the grasp
                of those
            Who much prefer to poetry
                plain prose.
        Of varied tastes indeed
            were all the five
        Companions, though most
            eager and alive
            Each in a way distinct to
                him alone,
            To view the noble city of
                Cologne.
            The doctor, stout and
                burly, hair quite gray,
Eyes sharp and keen, from which a merry ray

Shot ever and anon, was apt to **view**
The **whole** of life beneath the **rosy hue**
Of kindly thoughts with scientific **lore**
Commingled. Next the student from the
    shore
Of far America, that land of hope,
So large and vast that in its mighty **scope**
It sways the world ; and **men** of all degree
May feel **themselves** on those broad **acres**
    free.
Our student was a man of worthy name,
His sires of Revolutionary fame,
And in his heart **and** inmost soul there
    burned
Deep love of **country : though he sometimes**
    yearned,
As now, to taste poetic fountains **rare**
Of other lands than that he thought most
    fair.
Besides, he had a fancy **to** behold
Some records, and to hear some legends old
Of his Dutch ancestors, from whom he held
His home by every traveler beheld
Who journeys down the Hudson's lovely
    stream.
He had been charmed with Holland. Now
    his scheme
Of travel took the famed, historic Rhine.

And sober places which be deemed most
    fine
Not many months of time had be to speed
Along the way where errant fancies lead.
Each fleeting moment held an added zest,
And made him wish of sights to choose the
    best.
Of this quintette the third a matron wise,
From Boston, who with sympathetic eyes
And kindly love looked on the German dame
And her fair daughter, who but just now
    came
To join the others at Cologne. For friends,
In that true comradeship which never ends,
From early youth had these two matrons
    been :
Both widows now), and with them always
    seen
In youthful days the student's mother's frail
And lovely form, which withered 'neath the
    gale
Of fortune's changes later in her life.
When scarce two summers had she been a
    wife,
The doctor, too a friend of those young
    days
When lofty hopes and plans we always raise,
And everything seems possible for us.

Oh, that the strength of life came **then** !   For
    thus
Would **higher** ends be wrought and actions
    done.
Alas ! th' enthusiasm of youth is gone
When comes the wisdom of our later years,
Accompanied **by** self-distrust and fears
Which youthful hearts would gayly laugh to
    scorn.
Imagine then a bright and glorious morn
On which these five went out upon their way,
Through devious queer and narrow streets to
    stray,
Assailed by **many odors, good and bad,**
The latter far more frequently, 't is sad
To say, until upon their dazzled sight
The fair Cathedral, in the morning light,
Rose like a dream of beauty.   Pausing long
To see its walls and towers, famed in song
And legend, entered in our pilgrim band
At length, and putting slyly **in the** hand
Of **one** old sacristan, who stood about
And waited just to see **a party** out,
A fee which warmed **his** heart, they **went to**
    view
The Chapel of the Magi, where most true
Are skulls, and bones, and jewels rich and rare,
Whether or not the holy men are there.

Still, let us hope they did indeed find rest,
As meet they should, within the Church's
  breast.
Most interesting, too, the Devil's Stone,
Whereon are seen the marks his claws alone
Could make.   And this same Master-fiend we
  find
Plays still a part in every German mind
Inclined to fiction.   As to this fair church,
Traditions tell how sadly in the lurch
The foul fiend left the puzzled architect
Who tried to break his bargain, and detect
A way to serve both God and Mammon, still
A thing which men find far beyond their skill.
This tale the sacristan then told, and spoke
With droning voice, which sometimes hoarsely
  broke.

LEGEND OF THE COLOGNE
CATHEDRAL.

LEGEND OF THE COLOGNE CATHEDRAL.

ARCHBISHOP ENGELBERT, long, long
ago,
A mighty cathedral would have.
Calling the wisest of architects known,
He thus his commands to him gave.

"Build me a church of such beauty and grace
As never before has been seen.
Spare neither money, nor trouble, nor time,
But make it like visions unseen.

"Glorious let the spires rise unto heaven,
With gems let the altars be girt.
Thus shall great honor accrue to Cologne,
And the Archbishop Engelbert."

Gladly the architect went to his task,—
He thirsted for honor and fame.
"If," thought he, "this church should be a
success,
All the world will resound with my name.

" Not alone Engelbert, bishop and prince,
    By posterity far shall be known ;
People will proudly remember the man
    Who built the great church for Cologne."

Down at his task then he
    seated himself,
And traced a plan novel
    and fair.
"Ha !" cried a mocking
    voice close to his ear,
"That 's the Strassburg
    Cathedral there."

Back in amazement the ar-
    chitect jumped,
And vanishing out of his
    sight
Saw a small, withered, malicious old man,
    Who was laughing with all of his might.

Memory had indeed played him a trick,
    And that which he thought was his own,
Verily was but the Strassburg church,
    And not the new plan for Cologne.

" There ! " he cried out, as he made a new plan
    Of delicate, Gothic design.

" Nothing is like this ! I 'm surely this time
   Original in every line.

" Nothing is like it ! " he shouted in joy.
   Again came the voice at his side ;
Laughing and mocking the old man ap-
      peared,—
   " The Cathedral of Mayence ! " he cried.

Sad, but too true, and the architect then,
   With a sigh, drew another plan. " Ah !
This is my church," but again sneered the
      voice :
   " The Cathedral of Amiens ! Ha ! Ha ! "

" Who are you," cried out the puzzled young
      man,
   " That dare to make sport of my work ?
Can you do better than that yourself ? "
   And he threw him his staff with a jerk.

Quickly the old man began with the staff
   So novel and bold a design,
That the poor architect watched in amaze,
   And whispered : " That plan must be
      mine."

Ere it was more than half sketched, with a
      stroke
  The old man erased it, and said :
" There is a plan which will honor your name,
  And make you remembered when dead."

" Sell it to me," cried the architect, wild
  With excitement and rage and despair.
Mockingly, sneeringly, came the reply,
  In sounds which burnt into the air.

" Not for your gold," cried the Evil One,
  For 't was he, of course, as you know.
" Nothing care I for such trumpery stuff ;
  I 've more now than you ever could show.

" One price, and one only, I 'll take for my
      plan ;
  For that you shall have the whole."
" Name it ! Ah ! name it !" " Well, then,
      my son,
  The price I demand is—your soul."

Stunned and bewildered the architect sank
  On the ground, and a quick flash of light,
Blinding and reeking with sulphurous smoke,
  Took the little old man from his sight.

Horror-struck, home went the builder and
        prayed,
    But yet prayer relieved not his mind.
Then to confession he thoughtfully went,
    In hopes there some comfort to find.

Hearing his tale made the kind father quake,
    And yet, for the good of the town,
Sorry was he to lose such a church,
    When it doubtless would bring much
        renown.

Pilgrims in crowds would flock to the spot,
    And greater and greater would be
Yearly the annual revenues,
    That would come to the Holy See.

"Stay, my dear son," said the worthy old
        priest ;
    "I know of a scheme which to naught
All of the works of the Devil will bring,
    And frighten him quicker than thought.

"Take, then, this relic, a piece of the cross,
    And go forth without the least fear.
Fiends cannot touch you, or danger come
        nigh,
    While you hold what e'en devils revere."

Armed with the relic, that very midnight
    He met the foul fiend, and agreed,
When the plan, perfected, should be his own,
    He 'd sign, with his blood, the deed.

Stooping to find a sharp stone to draw blood,
    For neither of them had a knife,
Satan dropped, just for a moment, his plan,
    Which the architect seized, for his life.

"Satan, avaunt ! By this relic I charge
    You go to the place whence you came ! "
" Vanquished, 't is true," snarled the Evil One,
    But I 'll have my revenge all the same.

" *You* ne'er shall profit by this, my defeat ;
    And the church which you build from my
        plan,
Never while stars in their courses revolve
    Shall be finished by mortal man."

Thus with a flash and a groan went the Fiend,
    And nothing to this day is known
As to the name, the condition, and fame
    Of the poor architect of Cologne.

A silence fell upon the little band.
But soon the student quickly waved his hand,
As if to brush aside such legends old,
And, with a manner quite reserved and cold,
And tinctured with that scepticism which now
Pervades all classes more or less, we know,
But most of all the young ; the student said :
" No wonder that the minds which daily fed
On stories such as this should never grow
To any strength or power, but weakly bow
Before the fate which seemed to hold them
      bound
As in a vise. So on this holy ground
Six centuries this noble church has stood,
A monument to all that 's pure and good,
Unfinished. Now at last it seems to be
Entirely built, and so you plainly see
It only needed just a little strength
Of mind, which, happily, has come at
      length."
The sacristan smiled sadly : " Yes, my son,
The church indeed is very nearly done,
But after all, you see the marble floors
Are not quite finished, and the heavy doors
Which are to be the glory of the church
Have been delayed, from time to time. We
      search
In vain to find the secret of the bell

Which hangs in yonder tower. Its clangorous
    swell
Is frightful, yet the bell has not a flaw.
On this the Devil, too, has laid his claw.
Mark well my words.   They think this struc-
    ture will

Be finished soon.   'T is un-
    completed still."
And, with a shrug and goodly
    pinch of snuff,
The sacristan departed in a
    huff ;
As who should say : " These
    strangers in our town !
What right have they to pull our legends down
Or put our churches up, we 'd like to know ?
And I, for one, would like to tell them so."
The friends departed, with a smile, and went
To see the church St. Ursula was sent
To grace, with legends of her life and times,
Her faith, and love, her beauty, and her
    rhymes,
And most of all, her bones, and those of all
Th' eleven thousand virgins, of whose fall
Beneath the hands of ruthless Huns, brave
    tales
Are told, at which the stoutest spirit quails.

Full many other sights in fair Cologne
Our travelers enjoyed, each one his own
Peculiar thoughts put to the pleasure found
At every step, on this historic ground.
The trip up to the Alte Burg is one
Which never should a poet leave undone,
For here the tricksy Kobolds had their home,
And here they still believe the Kobolds come.
One little urchin, with a face quite pale
With horror, told our friends this grewsome
    tale.

THE KOBOLD AND THE BISHOP OF HILDESHEIM'S KITCHEN-BOY.

31

THE KOBOLD AND THE BISHOP OF
HILDESHEIM'S KITCHEN-BOY.

ROUND kitchen-fires,
  With vain desires,
    Roamed Kobold old and gray.
Some meat he took,
And so the cook
    Forthwith sent him away.

But this was naught,
The Kobold thought,
   To what the boy
       had done.
'T was nothing less
'Than dirty mess,
   Thrown o'er him,
       just for fun.

That very night,
As soon as light
   Departed from the sky,
The Kobold came
Up to his game.
   Revenge was in his eye.

33

That boy he took,
And with a look
  He killed him on the spot.
Then, for his sup,
He cut him up,
  And filled the dinner pot.

This awful fate
Came not too late
  To warn and guard the rest.
And, from that day,
The peasants gay
  Ne'er with the Kobolds jest.

A shout of laughter met the little lad,
Whose heart was soothed, and
    presently made glad
By several silver coins put in
    his hand.
This was a language he could
    understand
Far better than the mirth his
    tale provoked.
To him it was a thing not
    lightly joked
About, these tales of ghosts,
    or with a shout
Of laughter greeted.   Every
    lazy lout
Was threatened with the vengeance of the fay,
If his appointed task was not each day
Done well.   And every night some milk, or
    cream,
Or bread, was set aside, with childish dream
That possibly a Kobold might come by,
And, after doing all the farm-work, try
To rest himself, and take a little food.
Far better thus to have a spirit good
Attend one, than the other kind, which these
Become at once if we their hearts displease.

Another sprite which at Godorf one hears

Sad tales about, if e'er one
  interferes
With him, or follows his
  delusive light,
Is "Heerwisch."   Into
  many a sorry plight
He leads unwary travelers.
  His name
"Will-o'-the-Wisp" with
  us, his traits the same.
The peasants of Godorf a
  tale unfold
Of how a heedless girl the goblin old
Defied, and sang aloud this silly rhyme,
Which makes him madly chase one every time.

> "*Heerwisch! Ho! Ho!*
>   *Brenst wie haberstroh*
>   *Schlag mich blitzeblo.*"

> "Heerwisch! Ho! Ho!
>   Flare like a low.
>   Come, or I go."

On which the goblin followed her at once.
Ere in his face the stupid little dunce
Could shut the door of her own home, he flew
Within, with fiery wings, like lightnings blue.
The shock stunned every body present there,

As if a thunder-bolt in clearest air
Had fallen down.   As for the maiden's plight,
She never quite recovered from her fright.

   .   .   .   .   .   .

And now upon the deep and flowing Rhine
Our Pilgrims started, with this wise design,
To stop where'er their roving fancies willed,
And drink from pleasure's brimming goblets,
    filled
With youth's enthusiasm and manhood's
    power ;
So that each day, each swiftly flying hour
Should bring them joy which they could fully
    taste,
And not spoil all their trip, through too much
    haste.
Their first stop was a castle quite near by,
The German matron's, whence one could
    descry
The lovely stream, and here a day or so
They had the kindest welcome one could
    know.
For maid and matron did their very best
To show the greatest favor to each guest.
Where 's hospitality in any land
Found greater than from German hostess's
    hand ?

And for old friends, of course, the task is sweet
To give a greeting kind, and welcome meet.

．　　　　　．　　　　　．

Again the Rhine, and on its shores they
    passed
The ruined tower, all now remains, at last,
To mark the story of the wondrous harp,

Made from a lovely maiden's hair, whose
    sharp
Sad fate it was, to perish by the hand
Of her own sister. Love, you understand,

Was at the root of all the trouble sad.
The maiden fair a plighted lover had.
The sister loved him, too, so in the stream
She drowned the fair one, in the wicked dream
Of winning soon the lover to herself.
Her schemes were blighted, for some cunning
    elf
Made of a maid a harp, which, loudly struck
By clever wandering minstrel, brought ill-
    luck
To all nefarious schemes, and death to her
Who dared her sister's lover to prefer.

.   .   .   .   .   .

At Schwartz-Rheindorf, before they came to
    Bonn,
They paused awhile, and drew a peasant on
To tell the story of the convent there,
Now ruined, though it once was passing fair.

SCHWARTZ-RHEINDORF.

SCHWARTZ-RHEINDORF.

A Judgment against Gluttony.

THE Lady-Abbess and all her nuns
   Went hurrying down to the river.
For spring had come,
And the river's hum
   Had set the leaves a-quiver.

The Lady-Abbess and all her nuns
   Were watching the fish succumbing.
Two sturgeons fine,
Off which to dine,
   Were pleasure worth the coming.

The Lady-Abbess and all her nuns
   Had been most hard and snatching.
For many poor
They turned from their door,
   Because some of their fish they'd been
      catching.

The Lady-Abbess and all her nuns
　Took both of the two great sturgeons ;
In spite of the law,
When they plainly foresaw
　They 'd be sick, and a case for the surgeons.

The Lady-Abbess and all her nuns
　Were punished far worse than the fishes.
When down at the board
Were seated the horde,
　Not a vestige of fish in the dishes.

The Lady-Abbess and all her nuns
　Screamed with rage at the cook and the
　　　waiters.
" Oh, what have you done ?
Of the fishes not one
　Remains for your reverend *maters.*"

The Lady-Abbess and all her nuns
  Looked adown the shining river,
And away and afar,
Like the evening star,
  Shone the fish in the light all a-quiver.

The Lady-Abbess and all her nuns
  (For the convent should be an almsgiver),
Were judged so amiss,
That from that day to this
  They could catch ne'er a fish from that
    river.

"An awful warning!" said the doctor's
    voice,
As smilingly he wiped his eyes.   The choice
Of evils is but small, and yet I think
I 'd rather eat the fishes than to drink
A cup of disappointment like to that.
The fishes might have made them sick, but
    what
Would that have been to missing such a
    dish ?
I think we must forgive them, for the fish
They missed."   Then with a laugh and smile
    passed on
The friendly five, until they came to Bonn.
There was that dread tribunal's awful power
The Middle Ages feared, in troublous hour.
And here the robber-knight, Von Feyermahl,
Was brought to answer justice's noble call,
For running off with Kommern's lovely maid.
His life the forfeit which at length he paid.

  .   .   .   .   .

Beyond, the Drachenfels, where Siegfried
    won
The fame the Nibelungen Lied gives one
Who nobly earned it.   Here the dragon kept
The treasure of the king, his daughter, wept

As lost, until released and homeward led
In triumph. Gladly would the maid have
    wed
Her rescuer. But this was not to be,
For Siegfried, loveless, cared but to be free.

   .   .   .   .   .   .

The tale of Nonnenwörth and Rolandseck
Was told while passing, on the steamer's
    deck.

NONNENWÖRTH AND ROLANDSECK.

49

" HILDEGUNDA, maiden fair,
      Hildegunda, flower most rare,
May I on my helmet wear
Favors thine, sweet lady ? "

Thus spake Roland, knight of old,
Roland brave, in battle bold,
Yet whose heart, most strangely cold,
Ne'er before found lady.

Blushingly she answered him ;
Gave a rose ; her eyes were dim
With her tears, for life and limb
He would soon be risking.

In Crusades, far, far away
Sped the knight at break of day.
War is not a roundelay ;
Nor its fate worth risking.

Time sped on, and ne'er a word
Had the hapless maiden heard

For a twelvemonth, since had spurr'd
Far away her lover.

"Woe is me!" the lady cried.
"Roland surely must have died,
Else he would his promised bride
Send news of her lover."

In the monastery near
Sought she comfort for her fear;
Taking heavenward her career,
All of earth forswearing.

Came at last the pilgrim back.
Many foes along his track
He had laid full low, alack!
Danger ne'er forswearing.

Now, howe'er, before him loomed
Grief to which his life was doomed;
For no more before him bloomed
Lily fair, his lady.

Oh, the grief of that brave knight!
Powerless his strength and might
For restoring to his sight
Evermore, his lady.

"Gave a rose."

53

Opposite the little isle
Where the convent stood, a hill
Overlooked it, stern and chill.
There sat down brave Roland.

There he built of rock and stone
Tiny hut, for him alone.
Convent-bells of solemn tone,
Heard each day brave Roland.

Years passed thus, until one day
Roland heard the solemn lay
For a sister passed away,
Sung for Hildegunda.

Down upon the river's bank,
Worn and weak the warrior sank,
Passed from Life to Death's dark rank,
Joining Hildegunda.

Peasants sometimes hear the sound
Of sweet singing, underground.
Nevermore to part, now found,
Roland and Hildegunda.

A little silence fell upon the friends,
As when a touching melodrama ends.
But presently, with stories of the mine
Near by, which, haunted by a monk, whose
    wine,
If tasted once, strange fortunes brought to
    those
Who drank, our friends' bright spirits quickly
    rose.
This monk, or gnome is Meister Hämmerling
Called by the bards who of his prowess sing.
Soon by the walls of Hammerstein, the boat
Brought all our friends, where many an anec-
    dote
Of Charles Martel (the Hammer) one could
    hear.
Perhaps the name from iron-works quite near
Was giv'n, however. But Count Otto's bride,
Fair Irmengarde, and Henry Fourth, beside,
Are subjects certain to attract the love
Of all romancers. How Count Otto strove
To keep his lovely cousin for his wife,
In spite of Pope and King, and all his life
Devoted to her. Andernach which comes
Upon the view past Hammerstein, becomes
At times, they say, within the ruined walls
Of its old castle, such a scene of brawls

And shoutings, and such fiendish, ugly mirth,
Unseemly, wild, as never souls from earth
Could make. And strange, and fiendish forms
    and shapes
Are said to have been seen. The while es-
    capes
From ruined chimneys, clouds of sulphurous
    smoke,
To make the stoutest lungs fill up and choke.
And now Coblentz, and Ehrenbreitstein, too,
Across the river flash upon the view.
" Honor's broad stone " this fortress e'er shall
    be,
While German valor keeps that nation free.
And still beyond, the little island known
As Oberwörth, which had a house of stone
Upon it once, a convent. There was found
One spot so bare, 't was called the Devil's
    ground.
The awful tale a simple country lass
Here told our friends. We cannot let it pass.

THE DANCE O' THE DEAD.

THE DANCE O' THE DEAD.

HURRYING, scurrying, out from the light,
　　Blown about wildly by winds of the
　　　　night,
　　　　Grewsomely dance,
　　　　Retreat and advance,
　　　　Shaking their bones
　　　　Over the stones,
　　　　Laughing so free,
　　　　Yet without glee,
Dance on forever the fiends of the night.

Woe to the mortal approaching too near,
Letting the sounds of their mirth reach his ear.
　　　　Straightway he feels
　　　　Strange life in his heels,
　　　　And e'er he knows
　　　　Round him they close,
　　　　Leading him on,
　　　　E'er and anon
Seizing him, hurrying past with a jeer.

Into their circle at last he is drawn,
And long before the gray light of the dawn
  Scatters the host,
  All hope he has lost.
  Faster and swift,
  Now all adrift,
  Madly he whirls.
  Curses he hurls,
Yet by naught can the foul spell be withdrawn.

On and yet on whirls the dance to its goal.
Visions of blackness before him unroll ;
  All his misdeeds,
  With strange thoughts and creeds,
  As in a trance,—
  Still his feet dance.
  Sinks he, at last,
  Worn out, aghast,
And may the Lord give repose to his soul.

The pious woman crossed herself, and spoke
In awe-struck tones. At length, the student
    broke
The silence, calling their attention then
To Lahneck, still a frowning castle, when
The Templars held it as a last resort,
And perished nobly there, in firm support
Of what they held as right. Soon Rhens
    appeared
Upon the farther shore, and proudly reared
The Royal Throne, or hill, the Königstuhl,
Where Wenceslaus, the emperor, a fool
Indeed, forsook his lands and castle fine,
And sold them all for Bacharach's strong
    wine.
The Nixies' special home along this shore,
From warlike Boppart to the still St. Goar.
This martial Boppart, named
    for him who slew
His lady love, Maria, good
    and true,
Not knowing her in
    man's stout ar-
    mor dressed,
Until she breathed
    her last upon
    his breast.

And just beyond St. Goar, upon the sight
Of all the travelers, a glorious light
Fell full upon that rock, so closely bound
With most romantic legend ever found—
"The Lurlei."   At the very name comes forth
A host of fancies, proving well its worth.
And here, the German maiden, with a smile,
And modest hope the journey to beguile,
As gently up the stream they sailed along,
Told once again the tale, in sweetest song.

THE LURLEI.

HIGH up on the rocks, in the moonlight's
    gleam,
The Lurlei weaves her spell.
She is beautiful as a poet's dream,
    And she knows her power full well.

Around her ever there seems to play,
    Enveloping all her form,
A faint green light, like the river's spray,
    When it leaps up, soft and warm.

Her eyes are like stars of the brightest
        heaven,—
    Her smile like a magic wand.
Her golden harp, with its strings just seven,
    Hangs over the rocks, near her hand.

Her locks, of a lovely golden hue,
    Fall over her shoulders fair,
While a golden comb flashes through and
        through,
    And she sings as she combs her hair.

She sings a song of such wonderful power
    That nothing like it is heard,
Save the music, perhaps, of a man's last hour,
    Or the lilt of the paradise bird.

Once heard, it never can be forgot,
    That song so weird and wild.
It echoes for miles around the spot,
    And even the waves are beguiled.

Now woe betide the fisherman bold
    Or the knight of high degree !
If he hears the song of the sorceress cold,
    A lost man surely is he !

But who shall tell of the joy he feels,
    That strange, wild joy unknown
Save to him who with love of the Lurlei reels,
    Climbing up to her rocky throne.

Ere into the stream, to her watery den,
    The bright, mocking Lurlei leads,
Who shall say on what joys past human ken
    The soul of her lover feeds ?

But if the friends of the lost one send
    To capture the maiden fair,

" High up on the rocks, in the moonlight's gleam,
The Lurlei weaves her spell."

Far over the stream, with a mocking bend,
  She tosses her golden hair.

With a gurgling sound the waters rise,
  With a loving rush and swirl,
And carry away, before their eyes,
  The mocking, laughing girl.

And on the rocks, the very next night,
  The same as ever she stands ;
Still combing her hair in the clear moonlight,
  Or holding her harp in her hands.

Oh, how can one brave the Lurlei's power,
  How her charms and spells subdue ?
What will warn and guard one in danger's
      hour ?
  Will nothing betray a clue ?

As long as beauty and love exist,
  As long as hearts are warm,
So long will it always be hard to resist
  The Lurlei's, or beauty's, charm.

"Thanks, Mädchen!" cried they all, when
    ceased the song ;
While on them, and on all the shores along,
There seemed to rest the Lurlei's magic spell.
It stirred their pulses, young and old as well.
They listened for the echo, as it came,
Repeating ever Lurlei's magic name
Whene'er they called it.   Presently in sight
"The Seven Sisters" (seven rocks), whose
    plight
And fate were dreadful, as their hearts were
    hard.
They scorned their lovers' prayers ; this their
    reward.
As rocks, they stop and bar the river's way,
And rocks they will be till the Judgment
    Day.

"The Devil's Ladder" next attention claimed,
At Lorch ; for here a maiden justly famed
For youth and grace, was stolen by a gnome,
Because her father did not open home
And heart to him, a night or two before ;
And here the maid was kept two years and
    more.

At length a lover found a way to climb
Up on the rocks, and won his bride, in time.

At Rheinstein, too, full oft a tale is told
Of how a stratagem of lover bold
Succeeded, and how fast the maiden rode
Away from gouty bridegroom, to th' abode
Of handsome Cuno, where the wedding feast
Was eaten with rejoicing love, at least.
And now, at length, they neared fair Bingen's
    shore,
But passing first, at Bingen's very door,

The famous Mouse Tower, Bishop Hatto's
    tomb,
Where that unlucky man met justice's doom.
The tale most ably told in flowing rhyme
By Southey's pen, was read just at the time
Of passing, by the Boston Matron, who
Possessed a voice, well modulated, true,
And sweet to hear. The story is well known.
How Bishop Hatto fled away alone
To this, his fortress on the Rhine, because
He feared the vengeance of high Heaven's
    laws.
With promises of corn to starving poor
He 'd filled his barn, and then made fast the
    door,
And burnt them all, both women, men, and
    babes.
Although his conscience, blunt, forbore its
    stabs,
Heav'n's judgment came. A host of rats ap-
    peared.
They ate his corn, and straight their pathway
    steered
Toward Bishop Hatto's palace. Off he fled,
But they pursued him, and as quickly sped
Across the river, up the tower's wall,
And in at every hole and chink, though all

Were barred with greatest care. They gnawed
    their way
Through every fastening, without delay.

With sharpened teeth, they on the bishop fell,
And scarcely left one bone the tale to tell.
This Hatto must a wily man have been,
As by this other story here is seen.

BISHOP HATTO'S TREASON.

"HO! Archbishop Hatto!" cried Ludwig
    the Child,
Who in Germany ruled with a power far too
    mild,
"Will no one make way with Adalbert the
    bold?
This knight too much power continues to hold!
In spite of my battles he keeps me in check.
His forces are strong, and they come at his
    beck.
From his thralldom I 've struggled to shake
    myself free,
But Adalbert is still far too wily for me."

"Let me try," said Hatto, "I 'll punish his
    crime!
My life on it, I will outwit him this time!"
So, forth from the king's court he hurried
    away,
And reached the knight's castle with little
    delay.

Right humbly Adalbert received him, and
    said :—
"On an errand of mercy and truth are ye sped,
Holy Father? To Ehrenfels welcome full
    kind
Would I give to a man of such liberal mind."

"My son," said the bishop, "your king and
    your lord
Would fain be a friend to you. Put up your
    sword,
Make submission, and take then this boon
    without leaven,
The peace of your king and the blessing of
    Heaven."
With words such as these did the bishop pre-
    vail ;
And promised safe conduct, without the least
    fail.
"As sure as God liveth," the archbishop spake,
And his hand on the cross did not waver or
    shake.

"As sure as God liveth, I 'll bring you safe
    back
To this castle, and if aught of ill cross your
    track,

May the Lord deal with me thus, and more
  than that, too,
A thousand times over, if ill befall you."
Not an hour on their journey had started the
  train,
When the bishop put hand to his head, as in
  pain.
"You 're not hospitable to your bishop, Sir
  Knight ;
I am faint, and my head aches with hunger's
  might."

"Oh, pardon !   A thousand times pardon, my
  lord !
Come back and sit down at my well-laden
  board.
In my ardor of loyalty, ardor of host
Was forgotten a moment, though never was
  lost."
So back to the castle fast hurried the men,
Ate their breakfast and hurried away again ;
And by evening reached the proud court of
  the king,
At whose feet the knight hastened his homage
  to bring.

"Hold the traitor !" cried Ludwig, while
  Hatto stood near,

And saw the knight seized, yet did not inter-
    fere.
" You pledged your troth, Bishop," the baffled
    knight cried.
" But for you and your *honor*, I 'd not thus have
    died."
"And did I not keep it?" said Hatto, the
    lure,
" I promised I 'd take you in safety secure
To your castle. And did I not do so, my
    son ?
You asked no further promise. I gave you
    but one."

Then up rose the knight, and before to his
    death
They hurried him off, he said, gasping for
    breath :—
" My curse be upon you ! Lord Bishop, be-
    ware !
Both in Church and in State, a man must play
    fair.
My fate is most cruel, yet, if you could see
The future, which now is unrolled before
    me,
You would shudder and quake at your own
    guilty end,
For Heaven is certain its vengeance to send.

"You shall die by the teeth of vermin alone.
They shall pick your flesh from every bone.
And though, for mercy on Heaven you call,
Your voice shall ring back from a hard gray
    wall,
As hard and as cruel as is your heart,
Which by vermin and fiends shall be torn
    apart.
And through every age shall the story run,
Of Hatto, whose treachery 's equaled by
    none!"

A little farther on, at Rüdesheim,
They tell a tale of that unhappy time
When all the world crusading went.   The sire
Of lovely Gisela Brömser, from the fire
Of Paynim arms and slavery escaped,
Her future life against her liking shaped.
She loved a noble youth of high degree ;
Her father vowed the convent walls should be
Her future home.   At last, in her despair,
She threw herself within the Rhine, just where
It flows around the lofty castle wall,
And ended thus her griefs, and hopes, and all.
Her father built a cloister, to atone
For all his harshness, but his child was gone.
The peasants think her gentle spirit roves
Around the place, with voice like cooing doves.

Time presses us, to tell of Ingelheim,
And Charlemagne's adventures, love, and
        crime ;
Of Eginhard, and Emma fair and brave,
Who, maidenly and knightly fame to save,
Across the courtyard, where lay thick the
        snow,
Bore Eginhard upon her back, to show
The footsteps of one person only, from
Her chamber-window, issuing therefrom.

The monarch saw them, but he pardoned, too.
Their marriage quickly followed love so true.
And now to Mayence, with the two stone heads
Upon its walls, to tell of treason's deeds.
The Frauenlob, Von Meissen, lingers here
In memory and song so sweet and clear.
And, in the wall of its cathedral, there
Exists a fragment of the tomb so fair,
Erected for Fastrada, best loved wife
Of Charlemagne, who mourned her all his life,
Such influence she had o'er court and king.
This is the story of her magic ring.

FASTRADA'S RING.

87

FASTRADA'S RING.

OF all of the treasures Fastrada possessed,
    Freely giv'n by the love of the king,
The one she considered the choicest and best,
And prized above rubies, and all of the rest,
    Was the stone in her magic ring.

"T' was a curious stone, of most singular hue,
    And giv'n in a singular way
By a serpent, who Charlemagne's great justice
      knew,
And claimed 'gainst a toad who his nest hid
      from view
    The king's help, without any delay.

And justice was done to the serpent, who then,
    To show his respect toward the king,
Laid this beautiful gem on his table, and when
The king turned to thank him, away to his den
    Crawled the snake, leaving only the ring.

89

So the fair Empress wore it, and with it the love
    Of all who beheld her she drew
To herself, and her charms round the mon-
      arch she wove
So securely, that ne'er from her side would
      he rove,
    And daily his love for her grew.

But Death claimed Fastrada, so, under her
      tongue,
    She tried the rich treasure to hide.
O'er her perishing body the Emperor hung,
And to her loved garments he still fondly clung,
    Till torn weeping away from her side.

The archbishop, finding the jewel, transferred
    The monarch's affection to him.
He hung on the archbishop's every word.
In fact, this strange love was a trifle absurd,
    And did not pass away, like a whim.

So, into the hot springs at Aix-la-Chapelle
    The archbishop threw it away.
The people were charmed, for all chroniclers
      tell
How the king loved this city most fondly and
      well.
    In these springs the ring rests, to this day.

" This is her magic ring."

Would you know the bright jewel, which,
  polished or rough,
  Brings that love which Fastrada ne'er
  lacked?
You may find the gem still, if you search
  long enough.
Though it sparkles so brightly, 't is quite com-
  mon stuff,
  For the name of the jewel is—*tact.*

Still farther up the Rhine, and east, and west,
Our travelers found much of interest,
And fain would linger 'neath the magic spell
These legends cast o'er rocks and trees, as
    well
As on the far-famed stream.   A magic thrill
Ran through them all, a feeling of good-will
Among the elders, something more, perhaps,
With those two younger hearts, who felt the
    lapse
Of time less keenly.   For the sun of youth
Adorns and gilds with its eternal truth
Each day the happy lives it shines upon
And glorifies,—but more of this anon.

    .   .   .   .   .   .

At Heidelberg, with ruined castle crowned,
This tale, of truly heathen lore, was found.

THE PRIESTESS OF HERTHA.

95

THE PRIESTESS OF HERTHA.

IF faithless ever priestess prove,
   Or sacrifice to human love,
Hertha will be avenged.

So runs the law, yet, in despite,
One maiden loved a handsome knight.
Hertha will be avenged.

By sacrifices fair and sweet
They hoped the goddess's eyes to cheat ;
Hertha will be avenged.

Not long the guilty pair enjoyed
Their stolen love, for, while they toyed,
Hertha would be avenged.

Next day the lover came, to find
A sight which nearly turned his mind ;
Hertha would be avenged.

For o'er his love a fierce wolf stood,
And feasted on her heart's warm blood ;
And Hertha was avenged.

" Who wave their thin white veils
And dance upon the lake."

And now, within the deep Black Forest, glide
Our friends, where rocks, and trees, and
    lakes, all hide
The airy beings of th' ideal world.
If, in the " Mummelsee " a stone is hurled,
So great the stormy anger it provokes
Among the water-nymphs and fairy folks
Who live there, that they send a dreadful
    storm
Forthwith, and often do the greatest harm.
Here any misty night are clearly seen
These spectres of the lake, of witching mien,
The " Mümmeli," who wave their thin white
    veils
And dance upon the lake.   Full many tales
Of peasants there, tell how their lovers bold
Adore these maidens, stony-hearted, cold,
And sometimes follow them, when, at the hour
Appointed by their mighty master's power,
They have to seek again their watery home.
Such men, thus drowned, ne'er to the surface
    come.
Some lovers do not drown themselves, but
    wait
Upon the bank, until a much worse fate
O'ertakes them, lovesickness, and mad de-
    spair,
Until they end existence, starving there.

Of gnomes and fairies is the forest full.

Rastatt boasts a " White Lady's " spectral
  rule.
Near Gernsbach, the " Klingelcapelle " stands,
Commemorating rescue from the hands

Of temptress, in the form of woman fair,
Who once beset a pious hermit there.
The holy man was just about to yield
To her strong fascinations, when there pealed
A chime of tinkling bells upon his ear,
Which drove the fiend away, in greatest fear.

So once more with the shield of faith arrayed,
The hermit kneeled, and thankfully he prayed.

.   .   .   .   .

The Devil's Pulpit, and the Angel's, too,
Stand face to face, near Mt. Mercurius's view.
The Devil tried his best to argue down
The Angel sent to conquer his renown ;
And he, at first, prevailed, but by and by,
The Angel's arguments, so pure and high,
Gained favor, and the Devil fled away.
Both pulpits will stand empty, legends say,
Until the Devil finds a man who 's tried
To fill them both, and argue on each side.

.   .   .   .   .

The " Rockert " fairy lives near Eberstein,
And presents makes of food, and corn, and
    wine,
To starving but deserving poor, who love
To sing her praises through each dell and
    grove.

.   .   .   .   .

The legend of Alt-Windeck's castle old,
To all our friends, a queer old man there
    told.

ALT-WINDECK.

ALT-WINDECK.

A Warning to the Masses.

A knight of this castle imprisoned a dean,
    A popular dean of Strassburg.
But his people and friends would not thus let
        him go,
    This popular dean of Strassburg.

So, with peasants insurgent, they quickly laid
        siege
    To the castle, and would have succeeded
In forcing a way, had not strangely appeared
    A trench, which their pathway impeded

No mortal in sight, but a queer little hen
    Pecked away at the earth. 'T was a fairy,
Who flew to the castle, and there gave advice,
    With a manner most haughty and airy.

" Now, listen, Sir Knight, to a fairy's advice.
    Don't you see how much greater your
       power,
To league with the Church, and o'er clod-
       hoppers rule,
    When the clouds of danger lower?"

" True enough ! " said the knight, and he let
    the dean go,
    After entering into alliance.
" If the Church and the State together hold
    sway,
    To the people they bid defiance ! "

Our travelers would fain have lingered long,
Within this lovely home of myths and song.
Black Forest legends have an air of truth
Which comes from forests' deep perennial
    youth.
One feels that anything might happen there,
And love and faith and hope shine every-
    where.

But time is pressing, and we hurry on
To reach the great Hartz Mountains, and of
    one
Adventure, which our faithful friends befell,
To speak of, and its consequence to tell.
The scene, the summit of the Brocken, morn
The time, and here the German maiden,
    sworn
To secrecy, has started out to see
The Brocken spectre, if such chance might
    be.
The student, too, all unsuspecting, went
Up to the top, by path quite different.
The mists enveloped everything a while,
But presently the sun began to smile,
And far away a figure seemed to rise,
And come from out the misty, cloudy skies ;
A figure of a young and lovely maid,

But huge, gigantic in proportion made.
She raises up her hand and beckons. Lo,
Two figures now upon the cloud-mists glow.
The other is a man, who, standing, waits,
As if he saw beyond the pearly gates.
Yet not upon the wondrous, cloudy skies
Are fixed his looks, but on the Mädchen's
    eyes.
For there he finds the answer, long desired,
To most important question, love inspired.
Ah, well! 'T was only Brocken spectres
    heard
The words he uttered, or a passing bird
Perchance, who knew the old, old story well,
And none of these, forsooth, would ever tell.

Right lively ran the German matron's tongue ;
But love is love, and people will be young.
And pleased was she, the son of her old
    friend
Should seek her much-loved daughter's life
    to blend
With his.—And so, like shadows, come and
    go
The real and th' unreal, mingled so,
That through life's drama still the question
    spins,
Where ends the fact, where fancy then begins.

And, while we say "adieu," and from our
    sight
We see both friends and legends vanish quite,
We hope these lovers' lives as smooth may
    run
As sailed their boat beneath that summer's
    sun.
While still th' ideal world around may move,
The true ideal, that of faithful love,
Whether their home is on the Hudson fine,
Or, in the Mädchen's castle on the Rhine.

www.ingramcontent.com/pod-product-compliance
Lightning Source LLC
Chambersburg PA
CBHW032151010726
47493CB00008BA/2656